ADAM, ADAM, what Do You See?

This book belongs to

_____

To Bobby Tollison, our friend and pastor.
—bmj and ms

Text copyright © 2000 by Bill Martin Jr & Michael Sampson
Illustrations copyright © 2000 by Cathie Felstead

Published in Nashville, Tennessee, by Tommy Nelson®, a division of
Thomas Nelson, Inc.

Library of Congress Cataloging-in-Publication Data

Martin, Bill, 1916–
    Adam, Adam, what do you see? / written by Bill Martin, Jr and Michael Sampson ;
    illustrated by Cathie Felstead.
        p. cm.
    Summary: Presents, in rhymed and illustrated text, a variety of questions and answers
    about Biblical characters and events from the Old and New Testaments.
    ISBN 0-8499-7614-6
    1. Bible—Miscellanea—Juvenile literature. 2. Bible—Quotations—Juvenile literature [1.
Bible—Miscellanea 2. Questions and answers. 3. Christian life.] I. Sampson, Michael R.
II. Felstead, Cathie. III. Title.

BS612 .M37 2000
220.9'505--dc21

                                                                                00-036126

Printed in the United States of America
00 01 02 03 04 PHX 9 8 7 6 5 4 3 2 1

Bill Martin Jr and Michael Sampson

ADAM, ADAM,
What Do You See?

illustrated by
Cathie Felstead

Tommy
NELSON®
Thomas Nelson, Inc.
Nashville

**Adam, Adam,
What do you see?**

I see creation all around me.

Genesis 2:4–25

Noah, Noah,
What do you see?

I see animals in the ark with me.

Genesis 7:1–8:22

**Abraham, Abraham,
What do you see?**

I see a starry sky blinking at me.

Genesis 22:15–18

Joseph, Joseph,
What do you see?

I see father with a coat for me.

Genesis 37:3–4

Moses, Moses,
What do you see?

I see the Red Sea parting for me.
Exodus 14:15–31

**Samson, Samson,
What do you see?**

I see the strength God gave me.

Judges 14:5–6

I see a new land waiting for me.

Ruth 1:16–22

I see Goliath glaring at me.

1 Samuel 17:32–49

**Esther, Esther,
What do you see?**

I see the king listening to me.
Esther 5:1–8, 7:3–4

Mary, Mary,
What do you see?

I see Baby Jesus looking at me.
Luke 2:6–7

John, John,
What do you see?

I see God's Son baptized by me.

Matthew 3:13–17

Peter, Peter,
What do you see?

I see miracles all around me.

Luke 5:4–7

**Paul, Paul,
What do you see?**

I see an earthquake setting me free.

Acts 16:25–26

I see Jesus watching over me.
Matthew 19:13–14

Jesus, Jesus,
What do you see?

I see Adam, Noah, Abraham, Joseph, Moses, Samson, Ruth, David, Esther, Mary, John, Peter, Paul, and a little child—all seeking me. **THAT'S WHAT I SEE!**

Proverbs 8:17